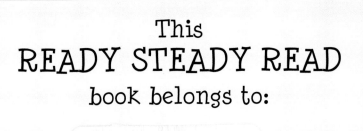

This
READY STEADY READ
book belongs to:

D0410077

My Reading Tree!

To Thomas James, with love
~ RS
For Mum and Dad
~ GH

LITTLE TIGER PRESS
An imprint of Magi Publications
1 The Coda Centre, 189 Munster Road,
London SW6 6AW
www.littletigerpress.com

This edition published 2008
First published in Great Britain 2001

Text copyright © Ragnhild Scamell 2001
Illustrations copyright © Gaby Hansen 2001
Ragnhild Scamell and Gaby Hansen have asserted their rights
to be identified as the author and illustrator of this work
under the Copyright, Designs and Patents Act, 1988
A CIP catalogue record for this book
is available from the British Library

Printed in China • All rights reserved
ISBN 978-1-84506-665-9

1 3 5 7 9 10 8 6 4 2

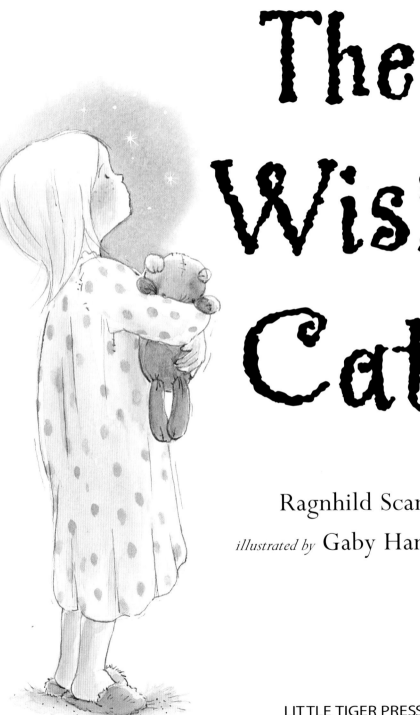

The Wish Cat

Ragnhild Scamell

illustrated by Gaby Hansen

LITTLE TIGER PRESS
London

Holly's house had a cat flap.
It was a small door in the big
door so a cat could come and
go. But Holly didn't have a cat.

One night, something magical
happened. Holly saw a falling star.
As the star trailed across the sky,
she made a wish.

"I wish I had a kitten," she
whispered. "A tiny, cuddly kitten
who could jump in and out of the
cat flap."

CRASH!

Something big landed on the window sill outside. It wasn't a kitten . . . It was Tom, the scruffiest, most raggedy cat Holly had ever seen. He sat there in the moonlight, smiling a crooked smile.

"*Miao-o-ow!*"

"I'm Tom, your wish cat," he seemed to say.

"It's a mistake,"
cried Holly.
"I wished for a kitten."

Tom didn't think Holly had made a mistake. He rubbed his torn ear against the window and howled so loudly it made him cough and splutter.

"Miao-o-ow, o-o-w, o-o-w!"

Holly hid under her quilt, hoping that he'd go away.

The next morning, Tom was still there, waiting for her outside the cat flap. He wanted to come in, and he had brought her a present of a smelly, old piece of fish.

"Yuk!" said Holly. She picked it up and dropped it in the dustbin. Tom looked puzzled.

"Bad cat," she said, shooing him away.

"Go on, go home!" said Holly, walking across to her swing.

But Tom was there
before her. He
sharpened his
claws on the
swing . . .

and washed his
coat noisily,
pulling out bits
of fur and
spitting them
everywhere.

At lunchtime, Tom sat on the window sill, watching Holly eat. She broke off a piece of her sandwich and passed it out to him through the cat flap. Tom wolfed it down, purring all the while.

In the afternoon, a cold wind swept through the garden and Holly had to wear her jacket and scarf. Tom didn't seem to feel the cold. He followed her around . . .

chasing leaves . . .

balancing along the
top of the fence . . .

showing off.

Soon it was time for Holly
to go indoors to tea.

"Bye then, Tom," she said,
and stroked his tatty head.

Tom followed her across to the
door and settled himself by the
cat flap.

That evening, it snowed.
Gleaming pompoms of
snow danced in the air.

Outside the cat flap,
Tom curled himself into a
ragged ball to keep warm.
Soon there was a white
cushion of snow all over
the doorstep, and on Tom.

Holly heard him miaowing
miserably. She ran to the
cat flap and held it open . . .

Tom came in, shaking snow
all over the kitchen floor.
"Poor old Tom," said Holly.

He ate a large plate of food and drank
an even larger bowl of warm milk.
Tom purred louder than ever when
Holly dried him with the kitchen towel.

Soon Tom had settled down, snug on Holly's bed. Holly stroked his scruffy fur, and together they watched the glittering stars.

Then, suddenly, another star fell. Holly couldn't think of a single thing to wish for. She had everything she wanted. And so had Tom.

Picture Dictionary

Look at the words below and put the correct picture stickers next to each word.

boots

dustbin

lamp

sandwich

★ Have you got these right? Then put a star on your reading tree!

Amazing Alphabet

a b c d e f g h i j k l m n
o p q r s t u v w x y z

Put the word stickers in the right alphabetical order, using the alphabet above to help.

home – lunchtime – cough – bad – afternoon

1) _____   2) _____   3) _____

4) _____   5) _____

★ Did you get this right? Add another star to your reading tree!

Cool Vowels and Consonants

The alphabet is made up of **vowels** and **consonants**.

Vowels sound soft. They are: a e i o u.

Consonants sound harder. They are: b c d f g h j k l m n p q r s t v w x y z.

1) Circle the words that begin with a vowel

ate	flap	open
crooked	indoors	wind

2) Circle the words that begin with a consonant

milk	purred	on
around	it	together

3) Circle the words that begin with a consonant and end with a vowel

evening	hid	splutter
go	made	the

★ Did you spot the vowels and consonants?
Add a star to your reading tree!

Wonderful Word Search

Find the following ten words in the word search below.
The words can be found written down and across.

cat	house	door
kitten	dustbin	leaves
fur	star	
garden	window	

F	U	R	I	N	D	S
N	D	P	B	Y	U	T
H	O	U	S	E	S	A
N	E	C	W	B	T	L
R	O	D	I	R	B	E
M	L	S	N	J	I	A
G	A	R	D	E	N	V
J	M	F	O	E	L	E
C	U	R	W	Q	K	S
A	O	V	H	S	J	X
T	K	I	T	T	E	N
U	P	L	W	A	Z	S
G	D	O	O	R	I	G

★ When you have done the word search,
add a star to your reading tree!

Sentence Order

All stories are made up of **sentences**. Tick the sentence below that came first in *The Wish Cat*.

☐ Holly saw a falling star.

☐ One night, something magical happened.

☐ As the star trailed across the sky, she made a wish.

★ Did you get this right? Remember to add another star to your reading tree!

Opposite Words

Match the words on the left to their **opposites** on the right. We've done the first one for you.

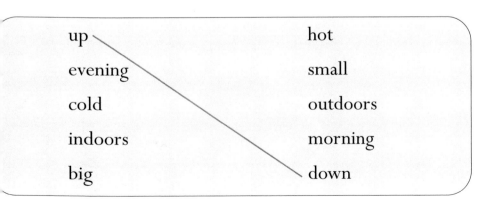

up   hot

evening   small

cold   outdoors

indoors   morning

big   down

★ Did you match the words with their opposites? Then add a star to your reading tree!

Busy Verbs

A **verb** is a doing word. Add the missing verbs from the **Busy Verbs** stickers to these sentences from the story:

rubbed – hid – danced – landed – wish

1) Something big _____ on the window sill outside.

2) I _____ I had a kitten.

3) He _____ his torn ear against the window.

4) Holly _____ under her quilt.

5) Gleaming pompoms of snow _____ in the air.

★ Did you get all the verbs right? Great!
Add the last star to your reading tree!